How to Write a Play

by Cynthia Rothman
illustrated by Molly Delaney

Harcourt

Orlando   Boston   Dallas   Chicago   San Diego

Visit *The Learning Site!*

www.harcourtschool.com

My little sister Jane couldn't go to sleep. My mom had to go into her room over and over again. Jane has quite an imagination. At first, Jane said she saw a monster. Next, she called out desperately, "Quick, Mommy! There's a big dinosaur!" Then she screamed for Mom because she was sure a huge bear was about to gobble her up. Finally Jane fell asleep, but by then it was really late.

"I'm exhausted," Mom said to me. "I know I promised to help with ideas for your play script, but maybe we can talk in the morning."

I was really disappointed, but under the circumstances I said it was okay. "I'm going to bed now, but don't worry, Mom," I joked. "I won't be calling you about any creatures."

Once in bed, I couldn't fall asleep. I kept thinking about all the choices I had been given for my class project. Why had I chosen to write a play? I didn't have a clue about how to write a play. What a mess!

"Why didn't I choose a plain old story?" I asked myself aloud.

CHOOSE A PROJECT

- Write a story.
- Write a play.
- Write a newspaper article.
- Write a poem.
- Write a biography.

"I beg your pardon," someone said. "Were you talking to me?"

"No," I said. "I was just talking to myself. By the way, who are you?"

"Don't you recognize me?" he said. "Look again. Notice my floppy hat and my torn clothes. Do you see the straw coming out of my face? Now do you know?"

"Oh, yes," I said. "You're a scarecrow."

"That I am, but not just any old scarecrow. I'm THE scarecrow." He smiled triumphantly.

"I'm happy to meet you," I said politely, "but what are you doing here?"

"I heard you were worried about writing a play, so I came to help," he said. "Now listen carefully. The first thing to do is to write a title for your play. Every play has one. The title should be catchy and grab the reader. Look at this one."

He waved his hands and a book appeared with these words on it.

"THIS is a great title, my favorite," he added. "Well, I've got to go now. Good luck."

Suddenly the scarecrow was gone.

"That was odd," I said aloud to myself. "Okay, I know that I need to think of a title for my play."

"I beg your pardon," someone said. "Were you talking to me?"

"No," I said, "I was just talking to myself. Who are you anyway?" My bedroom was certainly a busy place tonight.

"Don't you recognize me?" she asked. "Look again. Notice that I am very tiny. See that I can fly, and I light up. Now do you know?"

"Oh, yes," I said. "You're a tiny flying girl."

"That I am, but not just any tiny flying girl," she said. "I'm Tinkerbell."

"I'm happy to meet you," I replied in a friendly way. "Why are you here?"

"It seems that you are worried about writing a play," she said, "so I have come to help you. Just remember that when you write a play, you need a cast of characters. It's a list that tells who will be in the play. Look, here's one you might find acceptable."

She waved her hand, and a list appeared.

Cast of Characters

Peter Pan   Tinkerbell

Mr. and Mrs. Darling

Michael   Wendy

Nana   John

Captain Hook

"I love these characters," she said. "Good luck with your play."

I blinked once, and Tinkerbell was gone.

"This is the strangest place tonight," I said aloud to myself. "Now I will remember to choose a cast of characters."

"I beg your pardon," someone said. "Were you talking to me?"

I looked up and saw a young woman holding a cleaning cloth.

"No," I said. "I was just talking to myself. Who are you?"

"Don't you recognize me?" she asked, quickly pointing to the glass slipper on her foot.

"I do know you," I said. "You're Cinderella, but why have you come to see me?"

"It seems that you are worried about writing a play," Cinderella said, "so I have come to help you. The thing to remember when you write a play is to include the time and place of your play. Look!" She simply pointed, and a piece of paper appeared, pinned to a tree.

TIME: Long, long ago.

PLACE : The palace of the King and Queen

"It's important that we characters know the time and place where the play takes place. We need to know exactly where to go and when," Cinderella said. "Good luck," she cried, and she was off.

"How strange!" I said to myself. "Okay, I need to write the title, a cast of characters, and the time and place."

"I beg your pardon," someone said. "Were you talking to me?"

"No, I was just talking to myself," I said, looking way, way up. "Who are you?"

"Look!" he said. "Don't you see that I'm terribly big? Listen! 'Fee Fie Fo Fum.' Now do you know who I am?"

"Oh, yes. You're a giant," I said.

"I'm THE giant, Jack's giant!" he said.

"I'm happy to meet you," I said, although I was really scared. "May I ask why you've come?"

"I heard you were writing a play," he roared, "so I came to give some advice. One thing you must do is write dialogue. Dialogue is the words the characters say. First, write the character's name, and then write the words he or she will say. Look!"

As he shouted, a page floated down to me.

JACK: I hear something.
GIANT: Fee, Fie, Fo, Fum
JACK: I'd better find a place to hide.
GIANT: Where is that boy?

"Perhaps I was too scary in that story," the giant said, a bit repentant. "Well, good luck." He stomped off.

"There are quite a few things to remember," I said aloud to myself, "but I know I won't forget the dialogue."

"I beg your pardon," someone said. "Were you talking to me?"

I looked up and saw a princess. Again I explained that I was just talking to myself. I didn't want to hurt her feelings, so I politely asked, "Which princess are you?"

"Which princess?" she repeated, and then yawned several times. "Why, I'm THE princess, the REAL princess, the one who slept on a pile of mattresses to prove it. Oh, the injustice of it all!"

"Oh, I know you! You're the princess who couldn't sleep because she felt a tiny pea under a great pile of mattresses."

"That's me," she said, "but let's talk about your problem. I heard you need advice."

"Yes, I do!" I said.

"Just remember to write stage directions. You know that dialogue tells the characters what to say. You need to write stage directions to tell the characters what to do. Look!"

Queen: There now! *(placing a pea under a pile of mattresses)* We'll see if this girl really is a princess.

"Good luck," cried the princess, and off she went.

I could feel someone tapping my shoulder. I opened my eyes and saw Jane standing by the bed. "Get up, get up!" she said. "Mommy said to hurry or you'll be late for school."

I yawned and rubbed my eyes. "I'll be down in a second," I said.

I got dressed quickly and grabbed my book bag. Mom had fixed breakfast already. "Are you ready to talk about that play you're writing?" she asked.

Somehow, I didn't feel worried about the play anymore. I was thinking about my dream.

"I want to talk about the play," I said, "but first I have to tell you about my dream." I told Mom all about my dream, describing each of the characters who had come to visit. I told her from which story each character had come. I told her what each one looked like. I didn't really remember what they said, but I knew I had a long talk with each one.

Mom listened, smiled, and then said, "You always say that Jane has quite an imagination. Your imagination was awfully busy last night."

I agreed. Then I asked Mom about her ideas
for writing a play. She told me some important
things to remember. She said I should write a
title, a cast of characters, the time and place,
dialogue for the characters, and stage directions.
I listened carefully, but somehow everything
Mom said seemed so familiar.

Finally I said, "Thanks, Mom. I think I'll be able
to write that play today."

"Good luck," Mom said. I grabbed my book
bag, and in the blink of an eye, I was off.